Ab

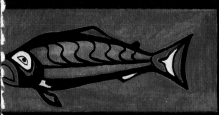

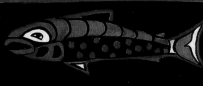
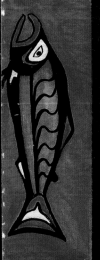

The SALMON
Twins

Written and Illustrated
by Caroll Simpson

H
HERITAGE

VICTORIA | VANCOUVER | CALGARY

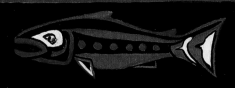

Long ago, on the shores of the Pacific Northwest, a family gathered to wait for the arrival of a new clan member.

MAY 1 5 2015

When the voice of a new baby filled the smoky house, the people cheered. A new child was important.

Greater joy overcame the village when the voice of a second baby joined the song of the first. The birth of twins was special and rare, and meant they could have Salmon as their crest.

"Children of the Salmon!" the people cheered.

"This is an occasion to celebrate," Father cried.

The new boy and girl were a blessing to the village.
The whole community gathered to welcome the Salmon
Twins and to thank the heavens for their good fortune.

The twins grew strong. Soon they pulled the white dog's tail and tipped over the water baskets. When they found **Woodworm** in the bottom of a box, both children wanted to hold it. They were surprised when Woodworm said,

"Beware of your greedy ways."

As the days grew long, the food supply shrank. The dried fish in the storage box was hard to reach. Only **Mink**, with its crafty ways, was full. With less food to share, the twins struggled and argued.

Mother told the children, "This is not the way of the people." But the twins did not listen.

Auntie told the children, "Stop your greedy ways and take the last fish to Grandmother."

But the twins did not listen. They pulled the fish apart and ate it up.

Thunderbird watched, and he was not pleased. Clapping his **great** wings, he changed the greedy children into a **Two-Headed Sea Serpent** and dropped it into the ocean.

It was a hard time for the people. They missed the twins, and the salmon were late coming up the river. Everyone understood there were lessons the children had to learn. The people also knew the twins were strong enough to find their way home. They hoped the salmon would find their way as well. Still, Grandmother often waited with Loon on the beach, looking for the children.

The twins fought and struggled
with each other and got nowhere. Sea Otter
laughed at their folly and said, "You must learn
to get along." Right away the twins understood.
They shared the body of the serpent.

Homesick, the serpent wished that greed had not brought it to this lonely place. It could not decide what to do. Finally, it decided to just go get something to eat.

But there were no salmon to be found, for deep in the ocean, Killer Whale guarded the gates to the Village of the Salmon. He was preventing the salmon from going up the river to feed the people. Killer Whale wanted the salmon all for himself.

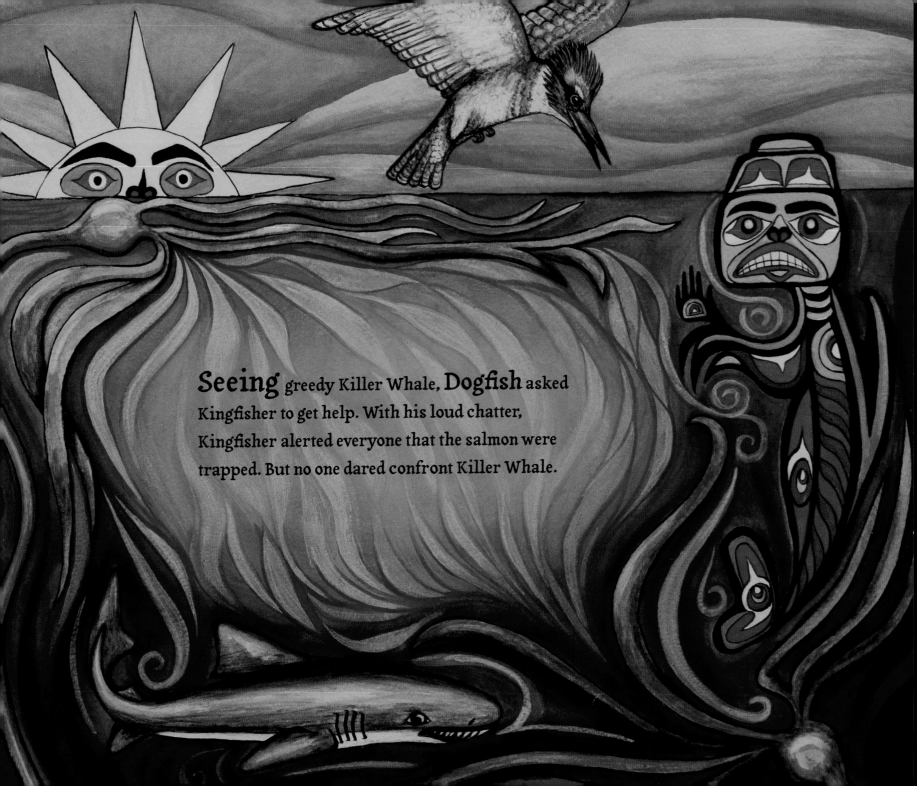

Seeing greedy Killer Whale, **Dogfish** asked Kingfisher to get help. With his loud chatter, Kingfisher alerted everyone that the salmon were trapped. But no one dared confront Killer Whale.

Night was falling when the Two-Headed Sea Serpent heard **Kingfisher's** story and understood why the people were hungry. Serpent set off for the Village of the Salmon, but travelling in the dark was difficult.

Swimming up to Gray Whale, the two heads of the serpent cried out, almost in unison, "Whale, Whale, please, please help us bring the salmon home. Our family is hungry."

Gray Whale closed his eyes so he would not see the eyes of the Serpent. He knew the eyes of Two-Headed Sea Serpents have many mystical powers.

Gray Whale was not the best friend of Killer Whale
and was glad to give Serpent a ride to the Village of the Salmon.
Thinking about the people going hungry made Serpent mad.
The faster Whale travelled, the angrier Serpent became,
thinking about Killer Whale's greed.

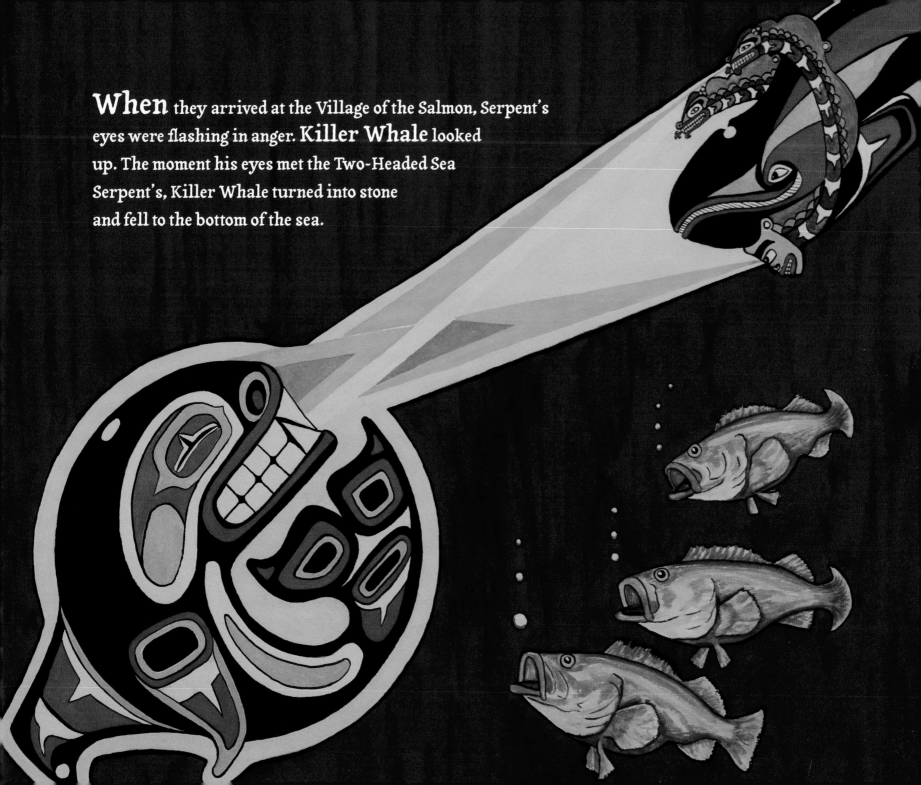

When they arrived at the Village of the Salmon, Serpent's eyes were flashing in anger. Killer Whale looked up. The moment his eyes met the Two-Headed Sea Serpent's, Killer Whale turned into stone and fell to the bottom of the sea.

Wasting no time, the **Two-Headed Sea Serpent** and Gray Whale drove the salmon up from the deep and to the river. Whale, of course, had to stop at the mouth of the river. The Two-Headed Sea Serpent quickly made a plan.

Working together, its two heads decided to spread their body from shore to shore to keep the salmon up the river where the people could get them. It would take days for the people to gather enough fish for the winter. Day and night, Serpent held tight to the shores of the river. This was hard to do. Halibut did not make it any easier by tickling Serpent's belly.

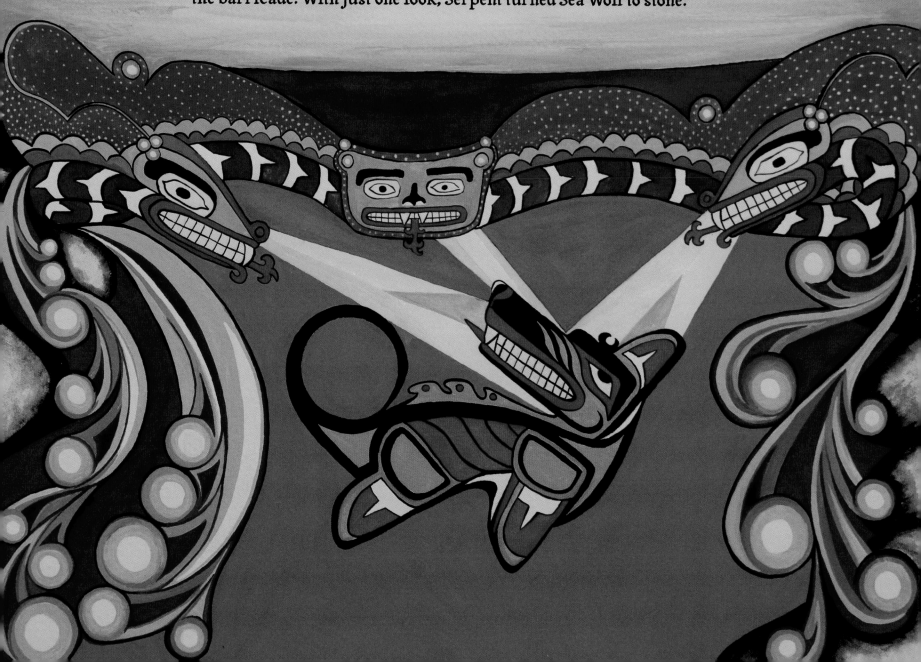

The Two-Headed Sea Serpent became exhausted and closed its eyes for a while. It almost did not see **Sea Wolf** trying to break through the barricade. With just one look, Serpent turned Sea Wolf to stone.

After a few days, Thunderbird flew over to make sure the people had caught enough salmon. When Thunderbird saw that the people had their full harvest, he clapped his giant wings. Instantly, the Two-Headed Sea Serpent turned back into hungry twins.

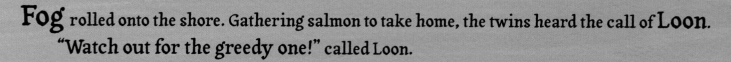

Fog rolled onto the shore. Gathering salmon to take home, the twins heard the call of Loon. "Watch out for the greedy one!" called Loon.

In the mist, they saw a big black rock move. It was Sea Lion, trying to grab their basket of fish. Already very fat and full of salmon, Sea Lion could hardly move. As the twins shared the weight of the heavy basket, they easily outran him.

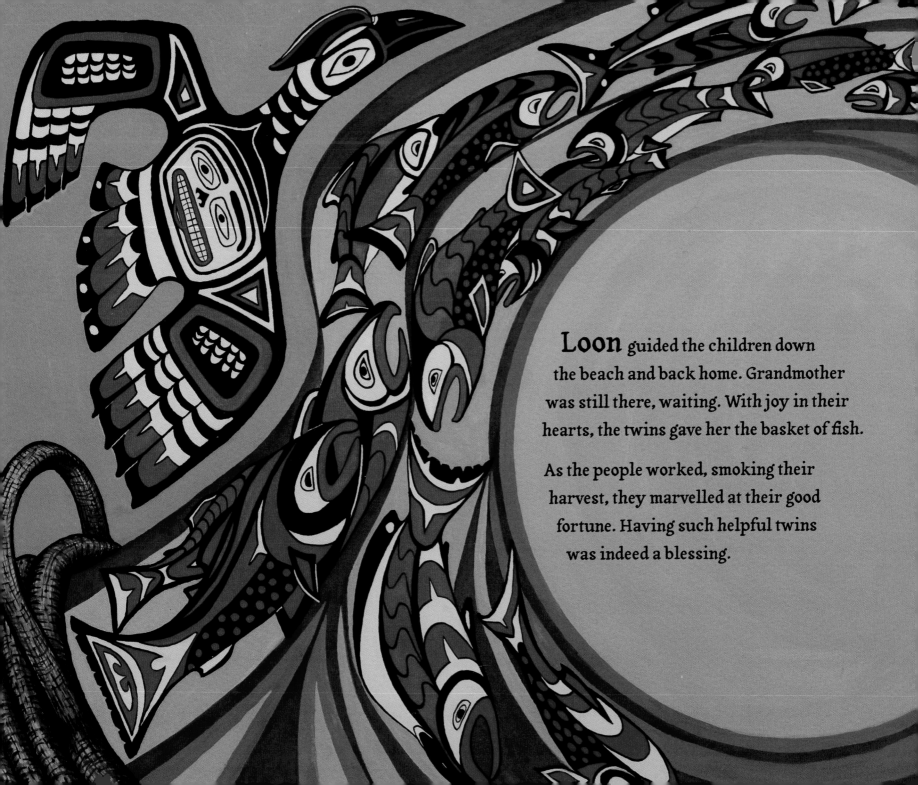

Loon guided the children down the beach and back home. Grandmother was still there, waiting. With joy in their hearts, the twins gave her the basket of fish.

As the people worked, smoking their harvest, they marvelled at their good fortune. Having such helpful twins was indeed a blessing.

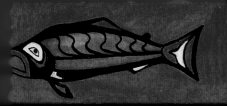

Supernatural Creatures

The coastal First Peoples were fortunate to live on the shores of the Pacific Ocean. Food was varied and abundant. This gave the people time to develop their culture and art. The most important event each year was the faithful return of the salmon. Without this reliable bounty, the winters would be long and the people would be hungry before spring.

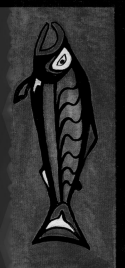

Dogfish are sharks. It is said they like to eat canoes. In images, they are shown with big foreheads and large eyes with vertical pupils. Their mouths are open and turned down, with lots of sharp teeth. They have slits for gills and two nostrils.

Gray whales use baleen, instead of teeth, to eat plankton. They were dangerous to hunt. The First Peoples gave great respect to Whale and carefully prepared for every hunt. The Gray Whale image has a large tail, a blowhole, a dorsal fin and a large, rounded head with lines that represent baleen.

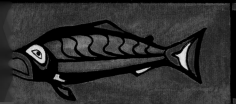

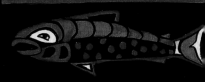

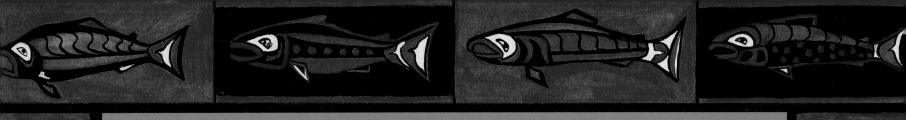

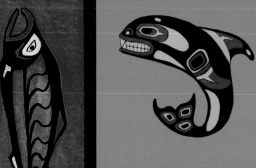

Killer whales are said to live in villages deep in the sea. They are great hunters and can capsize canoes and take people to their underwater villages. Killer Whale images are usually painted black and white and show a large, round head, many sharp teeth, a blowhole, a dorsal fin and a big tail.

Kingfisher is a blue, black and white bird that makes its home where there are fish and water. It has a loud chatter call and is an excellent and patient fisher. Kingfisher images usually show a heavy, straight beak, a short, heavy tail and a fish in its talons or mouth.

Loon is a diving bird that, legends say, once gave a blind man sight. In payment, the man threw a necklace of white dentalium shells around Loon's black neck. When it broke, some shells were scattered on Loon's back and some stayed around its neck. Loon images show the bird in a floating position, sometimes with young on its back.

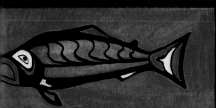

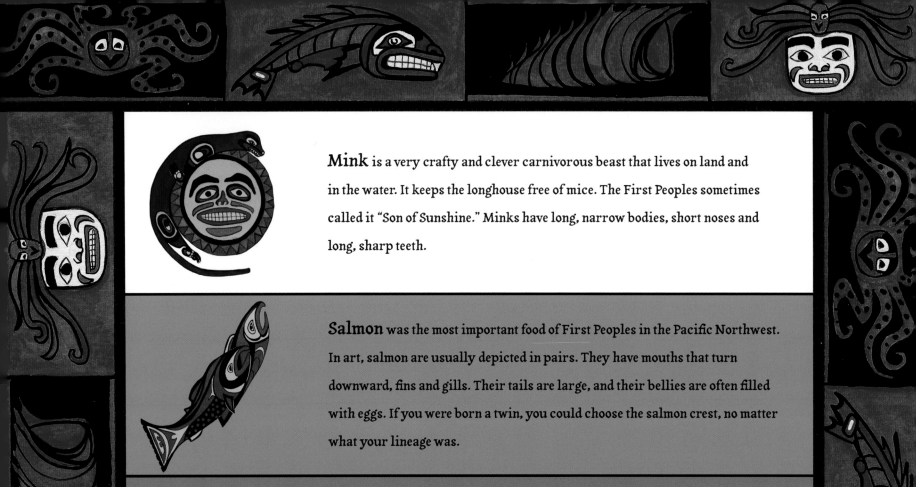

Mink is a very crafty and clever carnivorous beast that lives on land and in the water. It keeps the longhouse free of mice. The First Peoples sometimes called it "Son of Sunshine." Minks have long, narrow bodies, short noses and long, sharp teeth.

Salmon was the most important food of First Peoples in the Pacific Northwest. In art, salmon are usually depicted in pairs. They have mouths that turn downward, fins and gills. Their tails are large, and their bellies are often filled with eggs. If you were born a twin, you could choose the salmon crest, no matter what your lineage was.

Sea Lion is a skilled and respected hunter. The whiskers of Sea Lion are used to top the headdresses of chiefs. Some people say Sea Lion is the chief of the underwater world. Its image shows a large body, a full tail and strong front flippers. It has a large mouth with sharp teeth and small ears.

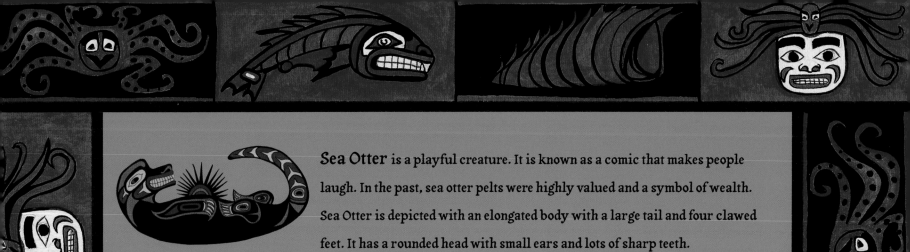

Sea Otter is a playful creature. It is known as a comic that makes people laugh. In the past, sea otter pelts were highly valued and a symbol of wealth. Sea Otter is depicted with an elongated body with a large tail and four clawed feet. It has a rounded head with small ears and lots of sharp teeth.

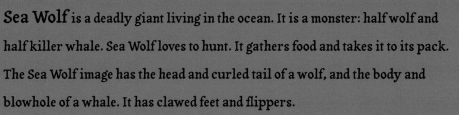

Sea Wolf is a deadly giant living in the ocean. It is a monster: half wolf and half killer whale. Sea Wolf loves to hunt. It gathers food and takes it to its pack. The Sea Wolf image has the head and curled tail of a wolf, and the body and blowhole of a whale. It has clawed feet and flippers.

Two-Headed Sea Serpent's glare can turn you into stone. The Sea Serpent image has two heads, one at each end of the tail, and a third face is in the middle of the body. The Serpent can turn into a Woodworm when it suits it. Woodworm has a gentle face with a sucker mouth and a worm's body.

Sea Life

All of these plants and creatures are native to the waters of the Pacific Northwest. They can be found along the shores of British Columbia, Alaska and Washington.

Bluefin tuna can grow up to 1.8 metres long and weigh as much as 140 kilograms. In years past, tuna as large as 4.3 metres long and 270 kilograms have been recorded. Sadly, these beautiful fish are in decline and may not recover.

Giant acorn barnacles have a grey/white shell, about 10 centimetres in diameter, and pink flesh. When barnacles die, their shells are used by small fish and crabs as little hideaway homes.

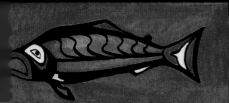

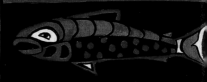

Giant Pacific octopi have an arm span of up to 4 metres. These giant molluscs are shy and can change colour to hide. They are intelligent and have a sharp beak for eating and for protecting themselves.

Leaf barnacles grow up to 8.3 centimetres long. They are sensitive to light—if a shadow passes over them, they shrink back. Leaf barnacles open at the top and use little "hands" called *cirri* to gather food.

Leather seastars grow to 20 centimetres across. If touched, they cast a strong odour. Under their bodies, they have a mouth and tiny feet that move them along. They eat sea cucumbers, anemones and urchins.

Moon jellyfish grow to 38 centimetres in diameter and float with the current. They have transparent, bell-shaped bodies with four horseshoe-shaped marks on top. There are toxic spears on the hundreds of tentacles around their bodies.

Painted urticina anemones grow to be 13 centimetres tall and have about 100 tentacles. Anemones grab small fish, crab, urchins and snails by using their tentacles, placing food into their mouths and forcing it into their body, which is like a giant stomach.

Purple-ringed topshells grow up to three centimetres wide. They eat plants and animals. To catch their prey, topshells rise up on their foot, spread their body wide and fall on top of the smaller creatures, trapping them underneath.

Purple sea urchins can live to be more than 30 years old and grow to nine centimetres in diameter. They eat plants and can burrow into solid rock. Most creatures leave the spiny urchin alone, but urchins are sea otters' favourite food.

Sea clown nudibranchs are sea slugs. They grow up to 15 centimetres long. If the sea bottom is rough, they rise to the surface and crawl across the underside of the water! Sea slugs are molluscs that have evolved to live without shells.

Yellow-eyed rockfish grow up to one metre long. They are sometimes called turkey-red rockfish or, mistakenly, red snapper. They are not red snapper. Yellow-eyed rockfish live in waters 35 to 365 metres deep!

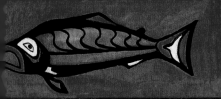
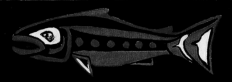

Heritage House Publishing Company Ltd.
heritagehouse.ca

Library and Archives Canada Cataloguing in Publication

Simpson, Caroll, 1951–
        The salmon twins / Caroll Simpson.

ISBN 978-1-927051-52-8 (bound) — ISBN 978-1-927757-00-9 (pbk.)

        I. Title.
PS8637.I484S35 2012   jC813'.6   C2012-901442-7

Edited by Grenfell Featherstone
Cover and book design by Chyla Cardinal
The text in this book is set in Yanone Tagesschrift and Gill Sans.

This book was produced using FSC®-certified, acid-free paper, processed chlorine free and printed with vegetable-based inks.

Heritage House acknowledges the financial support for its publishing program from the Government of Canada through the Canada Book Fund (CBF), Canada Council for the Arts and the province of British Columbia through the British Columbia Arts Council and the Book Publishing Tax Credit.

Canadian Heritage   Patrimoine canadien   Canada Council for the Arts   Conseil des Arts du Canada

BRITISH COLUMBIA ARTS COUNCIL

16 15 14 13 12 1 2 3 4 5

Printed in Canada

A Note From the Author

My goal in writing this book is to enhance children's understanding of the peoples who were here before European contact. I did not retell a legend of one First Nation. Rather, I wrote my own story of family and community dynamics, threading into it traits common to the supernatural creatures and beings of Northwest Coast mythologies. I also incorporated flora and fauna of the Pacific Northwest ocean. I hope this book will inspire young readers of all ethnicities to further their knowledge of and respect for all First Nations' culture, art, history and mythology.

Many sources inspired me, including the following.

Hilary Stewart's *Looking at Indian Art of the Northwest Coast* (Douglas & McIntyre, 2004) and *Looking at Totem Poles* (Douglas & McIntyre, 1993). Stewart's books are always by my side. She delivers clear and precise identification methods and mythologies. Stewart understands Northwest Coast art and her descriptions are extraordinary.

Indian Myths and Legends from the North Pacific Coast of America: Translation from Franz Boas' 1895 Edition of Indianische Sagen von der Nord-Pacifischen Küste-Amerikas (Talonbooks, 2006). Franz Boas wrote volumes about the First People, including a copious number of meticulously documented legends. We are fortunate to have access to these old records.

Bill Reid and Bill Holm's *Indian Art of the Northwest Coast: A Dialogue on Craftsmanship and Aesthetics* (University of Washington Press, 1975).

Bill Holm's *Northwest Coast Indian Art: An Analysis of Form* (University of Washington Press, 1965). Bill Holm has assembled criteria for anyone working with Northwest Coast art.

Cheryl Shearar's *Understanding Northwest Coast Art: A Guide to Crests, Beings and Symbols* (Douglas & McIntyre, 2000). Shearar's interpretation of First Nation art, legends and traits is an excellent compendium.

Pat Kramer's *Totem Poles* (Heritage House, 2008). This collection of historic totems includes legends, descriptions and locations. It is a colourful and informative reference.

Two good resources on sea serpents are G. Hawkins's "Prehistoric Desert Markings in Peru" (in P.H. Oehser's *National Geographic Society Research Reports*, 1974) and Roy Mackal's *Searching for Hidden Animals* (Doubleday, 1980).

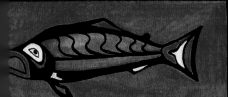

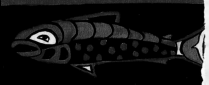